in

The Brothers Grimm
RUMPELSTILTSKIN

Illustrated by JOHN WALLNER

Prentice-Hall, Inc., Englewood Cliffs, New Jersey

Printed in the United States of America   ·J

Prentice-Hall International, Inc., London
Prentice-Hall of Australia, Pty. Ltd., Sydney
Prentice-Hall Canada, Inc., Toronto
Prentice-Hall of India Private Ltd., New Delhi
Prentice-Hall of Japan, Inc., Tokyo
Prentice-Hall of Southeast Asia Pte. Ltd., Singapore
Whitehall Books Limited, Wellington, New Zealand
Editora Prentice-Hall Do Brasil LTDA., Rio de Janeiro

10 9 8 7 6 5 4 3 2 1

Library of Congress Cataloging in Publication Data

Grimm, Jacob, 1785-1863.
  Rumpelstiltskin.

  Translation of: Rumpelstilzchen.
  Summary: A strange little man helps the miller's
daughter spin straw into gold for the king on the con-
dition that she will give him her first-born child.
  [1. Fairy Tales. 2. Folklore—Germany] I. Grimm,
Wilhelm, 1786-1859. II. Wallner, John C., ill.
III. Rumpelstiltskin (Folk tale). English. IV. Title.
PZ8.G882Ru 1984   398.2′1′0943 [E] 83-19100
ISBN 0-13-783747-X

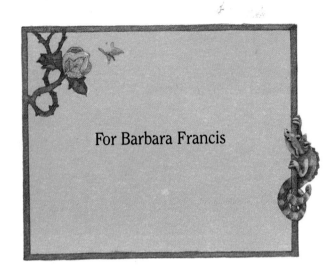

For Barbara Francis

There was once upon a time a poor miller who had a very beautiful daughter.

Now it happened one day that he had an audience with the King, and in order to appear a person of some importance, he told him that he had a daughter who could spin straw into gold.

"Now that's a talent worth having," said the King to the miller. "If your daughter is as clever as you say, bring her to my palace tomorrow and I'll put her to the test."

When the girl was brought to him, he led her into a room full of straw, gave her a spinning wheel and spindle, and said, "Now set to work and spin all night until early dawn, and if by that time you haven't spun the straw into gold, you shall die." Then he closed the door behind him and left her alone inside.

So the poor miller's daughter sat down, and didn't know what in the world she was to do. She hadn't the least idea of how to spin straw into gold, and she became at last so miserable that she began to cry.

Suddenly the door opened and in stepped a tiny little man who said, "Good evening, Miss Miller-maid. Why are you crying so bitterly?"

"Oh!" answered the girl, "I have to spin straw into gold and I haven't a notion how it's done."

"What will you give me if I spin it for you?" asked the little man.

"My necklace," replied the girl.

The little man took the necklace, sat himself down at the wheel, and whir, whir, whir, the wheel went round three times and the bobbin was full. Then he put on another, and whir, whir, whir, the wheel went round three times and the second too was full. And so it went on till the morning, when all the straw was spun away and all the bobbins were full of gold.

As soon as the sun rose the King came, and when he perceived the gold he was astonished and delighted, but his heart only lusted more than ever after the precious metal. He had the miller's daughter put into another room full of straw, much bigger than the first, and bade her, if she valued her life, spin it all into gold before the following morning.

The girl didn't know what to do and began to cry. Then the door opened as before, and the tiny little man appeared and said, "What will you give me if I spin the straw into gold for you?"

"The ring from my finger," answered the girl.

The little man took the ring, and whir! round went the spinning wheel again, and when morning broke he had spun all the straw into glittering gold.

The King was pleased beyond measure at the sight, but his greed for gold was still not satisfied, and he had the miller's daughter brought into a yet bigger room full of straw and said, "You must spin all this away in the night, but if you succeed this time you shall become my wife."

She's only a miller's daughter, it's true, he thought, but I couldn't find a richer wife if I were to search the whole world over.

When the girl was alone the little man appeared for the third time and said, "What will you give me if I spin the straw for you once again?"

"I've nothing more to give," answered the girl.

"Then promise me when you are Queen to give me your first child."

Who knows what may happen before that? thought the miller's daughter; and besides, she saw no other way out of it, so she promised the little man what he demanded, and he set to work once more and spun the straw into gold.

When the King came in the morning and found everything as he had desired, he straightway made her his wife, and the miller's daughter became a queen.

When a year had passed a beautiful son was born to her, and she thought no more of the little man, till all of a sudden one day he stepped into her room and said, "Now give me what you promised."

The Queen was in a great state and offered the little man all the riches in her kingdom if he would only leave her the child.

But the little man said, "No, a living creature is dearer to me than all the treasures in the world."

Then the Queen began to cry and sob so bitterly that the little man was sorry for her and said, "I'll give you three days to guess my name, and if you find it out in that time you may keep your child."

Then the Queen pondered the whole night over all the names she had ever heard, and sent a messenger to scour the land and to pick up far and near any names he should come across. When the little man arrived on the following day she began with Kasper, Melchior, Belshazzar, and all the other names she knew in a string, but at each one the little man called out, "That's not my name."

The next day she sent to inquire the names of all the people in the neighborhood, and had a long list of the most uncommon and extraordinary for the little man when he made his appearance. "Is your name perhaps Sheepshanks, Cruickshanks, Spindleshanks?"

But he always replied, "That's not my name."

On the third day the messenger returned and announced, "I have not been able to find any new names, but as I came upon a high hill round the corner of the wood, where the foxes and hares bid each other good night, I saw a little house, and in front of the house burned a fire, and round the fire sprang the most grotesque little man, hopping on one leg and crying:

'Tomorrow I brew, today I bake,
And then the child away I'll take;
For little deems my royal dame
That Rumpelstiltskin is my name!'"

You may imagine the Queen's delight at hearing the name, and when the little man stepped in shortly afterwards and asked, "Now, my lady Queen, what's my name?" she asked first, "Is your name Conrad?"

"No."

"Is your name Harry?"

"No."

"Is your name, perhaps, Rumpelstiltskin?"

"Some demon has told you that, some demon has told you that!" screamed the little man, and in his rage drove his right foot so far into the ground that it sank in up to his waist. Then in a passion he seized the left foot with both hands and tore himself in two.